THE SAND-HOG

BY

ARTHUR B. REEVE

British Library Cataloguing-in-Publication Data

A catalogue record for this book is available from the
British Library

Arthur Benjamin Reeve

Arthur Benjamin Reeve was born on 15th October 1880 in New York, USA.

Reeve received his University education at Princeton and upon graduating enrolled at the New York Law School. However, his career was not destined to be in the field of Law. Between 1910 and 1918 he produced 82 short stories for Cosmopolitan magazine featuring his super-sleuth Professor Craig Kennedy. Kennedy is sometimes referred to as "The American Sherlock Holmes" due to his astounding ability at crime solving and his Watson-like sidekick Walter Jameson, a newspaper reporter. These characters featured in 18 novels, some of which were pseudo-novels stitched together from various short stories.

During this period he also began authoring screenplays, beginning with *The Exploits of Elaine* (1914). By the end of this decade his film career was at its peak with his name appearing on seven films, most of them serials and three of them starring Harry Houdini. Due to the film industry's migration to the west coast of America and Reeve's desire to remain in the east he produced less and less work for film. However, in 1927 he entered into a contract to write film scenarios for notorious millionaire-murderer, Harry K. Thaw, on the subject of fake spiritualists. The deal resulted in a lawsuit when Thaw refused to pay. In late 1928, Reeve declared bankruptcy.

Reeve continued to write detective stories for pulp magazines, but also covered many celebrated crime cases for various newspapers, including the murder of William Desmond Taylor, and the trial of Lindbergh baby kidnapper, Bruno Hauptmann. During the 1930s he became an anti-rackets crusader and produced a work of history on the subject titled *The Golden Age of Crime* (1931).

In 1932 he moved to Trenton to be near his alma mater. He died on 9th August 1936.

THE SAND-HOG

"Interesting story, this fight between the Five-Borough and the Inter-River Transit," I remarked to Kennedy as I sketched out the draft of an expose of high finance for the Sunday Star.

"Then that will interest you, also," said he, throwing a letter down on my desk. He had just come in and was looking over his mail.

The letterhead bore the name of the Five-Borough Company. It was from Jack Orton, one of our intimates at college, who was in charge of the construction of a new tunnel under the river. It was brief, as Jack's letters always were. "I have a case here at the tunnel that I am sure will appeal to you, my own case, too," it read. "You can go as far as you like with it, but get to the bottom of the thing, no matter whom it hits. There is some deviltry afoot, and apparently no one is safe. Don't say a word to anybody about it, but drop over to see me as soon as you possibly can."

"Yes," I agreed, "that does interest me. When are you going over?"

"Now," replied Kennedy, who had not taken off his hat. "Can you come along?"

As we sped across the city in a taxicab, Craig remarked: "I wonder what is the trouble? Did you see in the society

3

news this morning the announcement of Jack's engagement to Vivian Taylor, the daughter of the president of the Five-Borough?"

I had seen it, but could not connect it with the trouble, whatever it was, at the tunnel, though I did try to connect the tunnel mystery with my expose.

We pulled up at the construction works, and a strapping Irishman met us. "Is this Professor Kennedy?" he asked of Craig.

"It is. Where is Mr. Orton's office?"

"I'm afraid, sir, it will be a long time before Mr. Orton is in his office again, sir. The doctor have just took him out of the medical lock, an' he said if you was to come before they took him to the 'orspital I was to bring you right up to the lock."

"Good heavens, man, what has happened?" exclaimed Kennedy. "Take us up to him quick."

Without waiting to answer, the Irishman led the way up and across a rough board platform until at last we came to what looked like a huge steel cylinder, lying horizontally, in which was a floor with a cot and some strange paraphernalia. On the cot lay Jack Orton, drawn and contorted, so changed that even his own mother would scarcely have recognised him. A doctor was bending over him, massaging the joints of his legs and his side.

"Thank you, Doctor, I feel a little better," he groaned. "No, I don't want to go back into the lock again, not unless the pain gets worse."

His eyes were closed, but hearing us he opened them and nodded.

"Yes, Craig," he murmured with difficulty, "this is Jack Orton. What do you think of me? I'm a pretty sight. How are you? And how are you, Walter? Not too vigorous with the hand-shakes, fellows. Sorry you couldn't get over before this happened."

"What's the matter?" we asked, glancing blankly from Orton to the doctor.

Orton forced a half smile. "Just a touch of the 'bends' from working in compressed air," he explained.

We looked at him, but could say nothing. I, at least, was thinking of his engagement.

"Yes," he added bitterly, "I know what you are thinking about, fellows. Look at me! Do you think such a wreck as I am now has any right to be engaged to the dearest girl in the world?"

"Mr. Orton," interposed the doctor, "I think you'll feel better if you'll keep quiet. You can see your friends in the hospital to-night, but for a few hours I think you had better rest. Gentlemen, if you will be so good as to postpone your conversation with Mr. Orton until later it would be much better."

"Then I'll see you to-night," said Orton to us feebly. Turning to a tall, spare, wiry chap, of just the build for tunnel work, where fat is fatal, he added: "This is Mr. Capps, my first assistant. He will show you the way down to the street again."

"Confound it!" exclaimed Craig, after we had left Capps. "What do you think of this? Even before we can get to him something has happened. The plot thickens before we are well into it. I think I'll not take a cab, or a car either. How are you for a walk until we can see Orton again?"

I could see that Craig was very much affected by the sudden accident that had happened to our friend, so I fell into his mood, and we walked block after block scarcely exchanging a word. His only remark, I recall, was, "Walter, I can't think it was an accident, coming so close after that letter." As for me, I scarcely knew what to think.

At last our walk brought us around to the private hospital where Orton was. As we were about to enter, a very handsome girl was leaving. Evidently she had been visiting some one of whom she thought a great deal. Her long fur coat was flying carelessly, unfastened in the cold night air; her features were pale, and her eyes had the fixed look of one who saw nothing but grief.

"It's terrible, Miss Taylor," I heard the man with her say soothingly, "and you must know that I sympathise with you a great deal."

Looking up quickly, I caught sight of Capps and bowed. He returned our bows and handed her gently into an automobile that was waiting.

"He might at least have introduced us," muttered Kennedy, as we went on into the hospital.

Orton was lying in bed, white and worn, propped up by pillows which the nurse kept arranging and rearranging to ease his pain. The Irishman whom we had seen at the tunnel was standing deferentially near the foot of the bed.

"Quite a number of visitors, nurse, for a new patient," said Orton, as he welcomed us. "First Capps and Paddy from the tunnel, then Vivian" - he was fingering some beautiful roses in a vase on a table near him - "and now, you fellows. I sent her home with Capps. She oughtn't to be out alone at this hour, and Capps is a good fellow. She's known him a long time. No, Paddy, put down your hat. I want you to stay. Paddy, by the way, fellows, is my right-hand man in managing the 'sandhogs' as we call the tunnel-workers. He has been a sand-hog on every tunnel job about the city since the first successful tunnel was completed. His real name is Flanagan, but we all know him best as Paddy."

Paddy nodded. "If I ever get over this and back to the tunnel," Orton went on, "Paddy will stick to me, and we will show Taylor, my prospective father-in-law and the president of the railroad company from which I took this contract, that I am not to blame for all the troubles we are having on the tunnel. Heaven knows that - "

"Oh, Mr. Orton, you ain't so bad," put in Paddy without the faintest touch of undue familiarity. "Look what I was when ye come to see me when I had the bends, sir."

"You old rascal," returned Orton, brightening up. "Craig, do you know how I found him? Crawling over the floor to the sink to pour the doctor's medicine down."

"Think I'd take that medicine," explained Paddy, hastily. "Not much. Don't I know that the only cure for the bends is bein' put back in the 'air' in the medical lock, same as they did with you, and bein' brought out slowly? That's the cure, that, an' grit, an' patience, an' time. Mark me wurds, gintlemen, he'll finish that tunnel an' beggin' yer pardon, Mr. Orton, marry that gurl, too. Didn't I see her with tears in her eyes right in this room when he wasn't lookin', and a smile when he was? Sure, ye'll be all right," continued Paddy, slapping his side and thigh. "We all get the bends more or less - all us sand-hogs. I was that doubled up meself that I felt like a big jack-knife. Had it in the arm, the side, and the leg all at once, that time he was just speakin' of. He'll be all right in a couple more weeks, sure, an' down in the air again, too, with the rest of his men. It's somethin' else he has on his moind."

"Then the case has nothing to do with your trouble, nothing to do with the bends?" asked Kennedy, keenly showing his anxiety to help our old friend.

"Well, it may and it may not," replied Orton thoughtfully. "I begin to think it has. We have had a great many cases of the bends among the men, and lots of the poor fellows have died, too. You know, of course, how the newspapers are roasting us. We are being called inhuman; they are going to investigate us; perhaps indict me. Oh, it's an awful mess; and now some one is trying to make Taylor believe it is my fault.

"Of course," he continued, "we are working under a high air-pressure just now, some days as high as forty pounds. You see, we have struck the very worst part of the job, a stretch of quicksand in the river-bed, and if we can get through this we'll strike pebbles and rock pretty soon, and then we'll be all right again."

He paused. Paddy quietly put in: "Beggin' yer pardon again, Mr. Orton, but we had entirely too many cases of the bends even when we were wurkin' at low pressure, in the rock, before we sthruck this sand. There's somethin' wrong, sir, or ye wouldn't be here yerself like this. The bends don't sthrike the ingineers, them as don't do the hard work, sir, and is careful, as ye know - not often."

"It's this way, Craig," resumed Orton. "When I took this contract for the Five-Borough Transit Company, they agreed to pay me liberally for it, with a big bonus if I finished ahead of time, and a big penalty if I exceeded the time. You may or may not know it, but there is some doubt about the validity of their franchise after a certain date, provided the tunnel is not ready for operation. Well, to make a long story short, you know there are rival companies that would like to see the work fail and the franchise revert to the city, or at least get tied up in the courts. I took it with the understanding that it was every man for himself and the devil take the hindmost."

"Have you yourself seen any evidences of rival influences hindering the work?" asked Kennedy.

Orton carefully weighed his reply. "To begin with," he answered at length, "while I was pushing the construction end, the Five-Borough was working with the state legislature to get a bill extending the time-limit of the franchise another year. Of course, if it had gone through it would have been fine for us. But some unseen influence blocked the company at every turn. It was subtle; it never came into the open. They played on public opinion as only demagogues of high finance can, very plausibly of course, but from the most selfish and ulterior motives. The bill was defeated."

I nodded. I knew all about that part of it, for it was in the article which I had been writing for the Star.

"But I had not counted on the extra year, anyhow," continued Orton, "so I wasn't disappointed. My plans were laid for the shorter time from the start. I built an island in the river so that we could work from each shore to it, as well as from the island to each shore, really from four points at once. And then, when everything was going ahead fine, and we were actually doubling the speed in this way, these confounded accidents" - he was leaning excitedly forward - " and lawsuits and delays and deaths began to happen."

Orton sank back as a paroxysm of the bends seized him, following his excitement.

"I should like very much to go down into the tunnel," said Kennedy simply.

"No sooner said than done," replied Orton, almost cheerfully, at seeing Kennedy so interested. "We can arrange that easily. Paddy will be glad to do the honours of the place in my absence."

"Indade I will do that same, sor," responded the faithful Paddy, "an' it's a shmall return for all ye've done for me."

"Very well, then," agreed Kennedy. "To-morrow morning we shall be on hand. Jack, depend on us. We will do our level best to get you out of this scrape."

"I knew you would, Craig," he replied. "I've read of some of your and Walter's exploits. You're a pair of bricks, you are. Good-bye, fellows," and his hands mechanically sought the vase of flowers which reminded him of their giver.

At home we sat for a long time in silence. "By George, Craig," I exclaimed at length, my mind reverting through the whirl of events to the glimpse of pain I had caught on the delicate face of the girl having the hospital, "Vivian Taylor is a beauty, though, isn't she?"

"And Capps thinks so, too," he returned, sinking again into his shell of silence. Then he suddenly rose and put on his hat and coat. I could see the old restless fever for work which came into his eyes whenever he had a case which interested him more than usual. I knew there would be no rest for Kennedy until he had finished it. Moreover, I knew it was useless for me to remonstrate with him, so I kept silent.

Don't wait up for me," he said. "I don't know when I'll be back. I'm going to the laboratory and the university library. Be ready early in the morning to help me delve into this tunnel mystery."

I awoke to find Kennedy dozing in a chair, partly dressed, but just as fresh as I was after my sleep. I think he had been dreaming out his course of action. At any rate, breakfast was a mere incident in his scheme, and we were over at the tunnel works when the night shift were going off.

Kennedy carried with him a moderate-sized box of the contents of which he seemed very careful. Paddy was waiting for us, and after a hasty whispered conversation, Craig stowed the box away behind the switchboard of the telephone central, after attaching it to the various wires. Paddy stood guard while this was going on so that no one would know about it, not even the telephone girl, whom he sent off on an errand.

Our first inspection was of that part of the works which was above ground. Paddy, who conducted us, introduced us first to the engineer in charge of this part of the work, a man named Shelton, who had knocked about the world a great deal, but had acquired a taciturnity that was Sphinxlike. If it had not been for Paddy, I fear we should have seen very little, for Shelton was not only secretive, but his explanations were such that even the editor of a technical journal would have had to blue pencil them considerably. However, we gained a pretty good idea of the tunnel works above ground - at least Kennedy did. He seemed very much interested in how the air was conveyed below ground, the tank for storing compressed air for emergencies, and other features. It quite won Paddy, although Shelton seemed to resent his interest even more than he despised my ignorance.

Next Paddy conducted us to the dressing-rooms. There we put on old clothes and oilskins, and the tunnel doctor examined us and extracted a written statement that we went down at our own risk and released the company from all liability - much to the disgust of Paddy.

"We're ready now, Mr. Capps," called Paddy, opening an office door on the way out.

"Very well, Flanagan," answered Capps, barely nodding to us. We heard him telephone some one, but could not catch the message, and in a minute he joined us. By this time I had formed the opinion, which I have since found to be correct, that tunnel men are not as a rule loquacious.

It was a new kind of thrill to me to go under the "air," as the men called it. With an instinctive last look at the skyline of New York and the waves playing in the glad sunlight, we entered a rude construction elevator and dropped from the surface to the bottom of a deep shaft. It was like going down into a mine. There was the air-lock, studded with bolts, and looking just like a huge boiler, turned horizontally.

The heavy iron door swung shut with a bang as Paddy and Capps, followed by Kennedy and myself, crept into the air-lock. Paddy turned on a valve, and compressed air from the tunnel began to rush in with a hiss as of escaping steam. Pound after pound to the square inch the pressure slowly rose until I felt sure the drums of my ears would burst. Then the hissing noise began to dwindle down to a wheeze, and then it stopped all of a sudden. That meant that the air-pressure in the lock was the same as that in the tunnel. Paddy pushed open the door in the other end of the lock from that by which we had entered.

Along the bottom of the completed tube we followed Paddy and Capps. On we trudged, fanned by the moist breath of the tunnel. Every few feet an incandescent light gleamed in the misty darkness. After perhaps a hundred paces we had to duck down under a semicircular partition covering the upper half of the tube.

"What is that?" I shouted at Paddy, the nasal ring of my own voice startling me.

"Emergency curtain," he shouted back.

Words were economised. Later, I learned that should the tunnel start to flood, the other half of the emergency curtain could be dropped so as to cut off the inrushing water.

Men passed, pushing little cars full of "muck" or sand taken out from before the "shield" - which is the head by which this mechanical mole advances under the river-bed. These men and others who do the shovelling are the "muckers."

Pipes laid along the side of the tunnel conducted compressed air and fresh water, while electric light and telephone wires were strung all about. These and the tools and other things strewn along the tunnel obstructed the narrow passage to such an extent that we had to be careful in picking our way.

At last we reached the shield, and on hands and knees we crawled out into one of its compartments. Here we experienced for the first time the weird realisation that only the "air" stood between us and destruction from the tons and tons of sand and water overhead. At some points in the sand we could feel the air escaping, which appeared at the surface of the river overhead in bubbles, indicating to those passing in the river boats just how far each tunnel heading below had proceeded. When the loss of air became too great, I learned, scows would dump hundreds of tons of clay overhead to make an artificial river bed for the shield to stick its nose safely through, for if the river bed became too thin overhead the "air" would blow a hole in it.

Capps, it seemed to me, was unusually anxious to have the visit over. At any rate, while Kennedy and Paddy were still crawling about the shield, he stood aside, now and then giving the men an order and apparently forgetful of us.

My own curiosity was quickly satisfied, and I sat down on a pile of the segments out of which the successive rings of the tunnel were made. As I sat there waiting for Kennedy, I absently reached into my pocket and pulled out a cigarette and lighted it. It burned amazingly fast, as if it were made of tinder, the reason being the excess of oxygen in the compressed air. I was looking at it in astonishment, when suddenly I felt a blow on my hand. It was Capps.

"You chump!" he shouted as he ground the cigarette under his boot. "Don't you know it is dangerous to smoke in compressed air?"

"Why, no," I replied, smothering my anger at his manner. "No one said anything about it."

"Well, it is dangerous, and Orton's a fool to let greenhorns come in here."

"And to whom may it be dangerous?" I heard a voice inquire over my shoulder. It was Kennedy. "To Mr. Jameson or the rest of us?"

"Well," answered Capps, "I supposed everybody knew it was reckless, and that he would hurt himself more by one smoke in the air than by a hundred up above. That's all."

He turned on Kennedy sullenly, and started to walk back up the tunnel. But I could not help thinking that his manner was anything but solicitude for my own health. I could just barely catch his words over the tunnel telephone some feet away. I thought he said that everything was going along all right and that he was about to start back again. Then he disappeared in the mist of the tube without even nodding a farewell.

Kennedy and I remained standing, not far from the outlet of the pipe by which the compressed air was being supplied in the tunnel from the compressors above, in order to keep the pressure up to the constant level necessary. I saw Kennedy give a hurried glance about, as if to note whether any one were looking at us. No one was. With a quick motion he reached down. In his hand was a stout little glass flask with a tight-fitting metal top. For a second he held it near the outlet of the pipe; then he snapped the top shut and slipped it back into his pocket as quickly as he had produced it.

Slowly we commenced to retrace our steps to the airlock, our curiosity satisfied by this glimpse of one of the most remarkable developments of modern engineering.

"Where's Paddy?" asked Kennedy, stopping suddenly. "We've forgotten him."

"Back there at the shield, I suppose," said I. "Let's whistle and attract his attention.

I pursed up my lips, but if I had been whistling for a million dollars I couldn't have done it.

Craig laughed. "Walter, you are indeed learning many strange things. You can't whistle in compressed air.

I was too chagrined to answer. First it was Capps; now it was my own friend Kennedy chaffing me for my ignorance. I was glad to see Paddy's huge form looming in the semi-darkness. He had seen that we were gone and hurried after us.

"Won't ye stay down an' see some more, gintlemen?" he asked. "Or have ye had enough of the air? It seems very smelly to me this mornin' - I don't blame ye. I guess them as doesn't have to stay here is satisfied with a few minutes of it."

"No, thanks, I guess we needn't stay down any longer," replied Craig. "I think I have seen all that is necessary - at least for the present. Capps has gone out ahead of us. I think you can take us out now, Paddy. I would much rather have you do it than to go with anybody else."

Coming out, I found, was really more dangerous than going in, for it is while coming out of the that men are liable to get the bends. Roughly, half a minute should be consumed in coming out from each pound of pressure, though for such high pressures as we had been under, considerably more time was required in order to do it safely. We spent about half an hour in the air-lock, I should judge.

Paddy let the air out of the lock by turning on a valve leading to the outside, normal atmosphere. Thus he let the air out rapidly at first until we had got down to half the pressure of the tunnel. The second half he did slowly, and it was indeed tedious, but it was safe. There was at first a hissing sound when he opened the valve, and it grew colder in the lock, since air absorbs heat from surrounding objects when it expands. We were glad to draw sweaters on over our heads. It also grew as misty as a London fog as the water-vapour in the air was condensed.

At last the hiss of escaping air ceased. The door to the modern dungeon of science grated open. We walked out of the lock to the elevator shaft and were hoisted up to God's air again. We gazed out across the river with its waves dancing in the sunlight. There, out in the middle, was a wreath of bubbles on the water. That marked the end of the tunnel, over the shield. Down beneath those bubbles the sand-hogs were rooting. But what was the mystery that the tunnel held in its dark, dank bosom? Had Kennedy a clue?

"I think we had better wait around a bit," remarked Kennedy, as we sipped our hot coffee in the dressing-room and warmed ourselves from the chill of coming out of the lock. "In case anything should happen to us and we should get the bends this is the place for us, near the medical lock, as it is called - that big steel cylinder over there, where we found Orton. The best cure for the bends is to go back under the air-recompression they call it. The renewed pressure causes the gas in the blood to contract again, and thus it is eliminated - sometimes. At any rate, it is the best-known cure and considerably reduces the pain in the worst cases. When you have a bad case like Orton's it means that the damage is done; the gas has ruptured some veins. Paddy was right. Only time will cure that."

Nothing happened to us, however, and in a couple of hours we dropped in on Orton at the hospital where he was slowly convalescing.

"What do you think of the case?" he asked anxiously.

"Nothing as yet," replied Craig, "but I have set certain things in motion which will give us a pretty good line on what is taking place in a day or so."

Orton's face fell, but he said nothing. He bit his lip nervously and looked out of the sun-parlour at the roofs of New York around him.

"What has happened since last night to increase your anxiety, Jack?" asked Craig sympathetically. Orton wheeled his chair about slowly, faced us, and drew a letter from his pocket. Laying it flat on the table he covered the lower part with the envelope.

"Read that," he said.

"Dear Jack," it began. I saw at once that it was from Miss Taylor. "Just a line," she wrote, "to let you know that I am thinking about you always and hoping that you are better than when I saw you this evening. Papa had the chairman of the board of directors of the Five-Borough here late to-night, and they were in the library for over an hour. For your sake, Jack, I played the eavesdropper, but they talked so low that I could hear nothing, though I know they were talking about you and the tunnel. When they came out, I had no time to escape, so I slipped behind a portiere. I heard father say: 'Yes, I guess you are right, Morris. The thing has gone on long enough. If there is one more big accident we shall have to compromise with the Inter-River and carry on the work jointly. We have given Orton his chance, and if they demand that this other fellow shall be put in, I suppose we shall have to concede it.' Mr. Morris seemed pleased that father agreed with him and said so. Oh, Jack, can't you do something to show them they are wrong, and do it quickly? I never miss an opportunity of telling papa it is not your fault that all these delays take place."

The rest of the letter was covered by the envelope, and Orton would not have shown it for worlds.

21

"Orton," said Kennedy, after a few moments' reflection, "I will take a chance for your sake - a long chance, but I think a good one. If you can pull yourself together by this afternoon, be over at your office at four. Be sure to have Shelton and Capps there, and you can tell Mr. Taylor that you have something very important to set before him. Now, I must hurry if I am to fulfil my part of the contract. Goodbye, Jack. Keep a stiff upper lip, old man. I'll have something that will surprise you this afternoon."

Outside, as he hurried uptown, Craig was silent, but I could see his features working nervously, and as we parted he merely said: "Of course, you'll be there, Walter. I'll put the finishing touches on your story of high finance."

Slowly enough the few hours passed before I found myself again in Orton's office. He was there already, despite the orders of his physician, who was disgusted at this excursion from the hospital. Kennedy was there, too, grim and silent. We sat watching the two indicators beside Orton's desk, which showed the air pressure in the two tubes. The needles were vibrating ever so little and tracing a red-ink line on the ruled paper that unwound from the drum. From the moment the tunnels were started, here was preserved a faithful record of every slightest variation of air pressure.

"Telephone down into the tube and have Capps come up," said Craig at length, glancing at Orton's desk clock.

"Taylor will be here pretty soon, and I want Capps to be out of the tunnel by the time he comes. Then get Shelton, too."

In response to Orton's summons Capps and Shelton came into the office, just as a large town car pulled up outside the tunnel works. A tall, distinguished-looking man stepped out and turned again toward the door of the car.

"There's Taylor," I remarked, for I had seen him often at investigations before the Public Service Commission.

"And Vivian, too," exclaimed Orton excitedly. "Say, fellows, clear off these desks. Quick, before she gets up here. In the closet with these blueprints, Walter. There, that's a little better. If I had known she was coming I would at least have had the place swept out. Puff! look at the dust on this desk of mine. Well, there's no help for it. There they are at the door now. Why, Vivian, what a surprise."

"Jack!" she exclaimed, almost ignoring the rest of us and quickly crossing to his chair to lay a restraining hand on his shoulder as he vainly tried to stand up to welcome her.

"Why didn't you tell me you were coming?" he asked eagerly. "I would have had the place fixed up a bit."

I prefer it this way," she said, looking curiously around at the samples of tunnel paraphernalia and the charts and diagrams on the walls.

"Yes, Orton," said President Taylor, "she would come - dropped in at the office and when I tried to excuse myself for a business appointment, demanded which way I was going.

When I said I was coming here, she insisted on coming, too."

Orton smiled. He knew that she had taken this simple and direct means of being there, but he said nothing, and merely introduced us to the president and Miss Taylor.

An awkward silence followed. Orton cleared his throat. "I think you all know why we are here," he began. "We have been and are having altogether too many accidents in the tunnel, too many cases of the bends, too many deaths, too many delays to the work. Well - er - I - er - Mr. Kennedy has something to say about them, I believe."

No sound was heard save the vibration of the air-compressors and an occasional shout of a workman at the shaft leading down to the air-locks.

"There is no need for me to say anything about caisson disease to you, gentlemen, or to you, Miss Taylor," began Kennedy. "I think you all know how it is caused and a good deal about it already. But, to be perfectly clear, I will say that there are live things that must, above all others, be looked after in tunnel work: the air pressure, the amount of carbon dioxide in the air, the length of the shifts which the men work, the state of health of the men as near as physical examination can determine it, and the rapidity with which the men come out of the air, so as to prevent carelessness which may cause the bends.

"I find," he continued, "that the air pressure is not too high for safety. Proper examinations for carbon dioxide are made, and the amount in the air is not excessive. The shifts are not even as long as those prescribed by the law. The medical inspection is quite adequate and as for the time taken in coming out through the locks the rules are stringent."

A look of relief crossed the face of Orton at this commendation of his work, followed by a puzzled expression that plainly indicated that he would like to know what was the matter, if all the crucial things were all right.

"But," resumed Kennedy, "the bends are still hitting the men, and there is no telling when a fire or a blow-out may occur in any of the eight headings that are now being pushed under the river. Quite often the work has been delayed and the tunnel partly or wholly flooded. Now, you know the theory of the bends. It is that air - mostly the nitrogen in the air - is absorbed by the blood under the pressure. In coming out of the 'air' if the nitrogen is not all eliminated, it stays in the blood and, as the pressure is reduced, it expands. It is just as if you take a bottle of charged water and pull the cork suddenly. The gas rises in big bubbles. Cork it again and the gas bubbles cease to rise and finally disappear. If you make a pin-hole in the cork the gas will escape slowly, without a bubble. You must decompress the human body slowly, by stages, to let the super-saturated blood give up its nitrogen to the lungs, which can eliminate it. Otherwise these bubbles catch in the veins, and the result is severe pains, paralysis, and even death. Gentlemen, I see that I am just wasting time telling you this, for you know it all well. But consider."

Kennedy placed an empty corked flask on the table. The others regarded it curiously, but I recalled having seen it in the tunnel.

"In this bottle," explained Kennedy, "I collected some of the air from the tunnel when I was down there this morning. I have since analysed it. The quantity of carbon dioxide is approximately what it should be - not high enough of itself to cause trouble. But," he spoke slowly to emphasise his words, " I found something else in that air beside carbon dioxide."

"Nitrogen?" broke in Orton quickly, leaning forward.

"Of course; it is a constituent of air. But that is not what I mean."

"Then, for Heaven's sake, what did you find?" asked Orton.

"I found in this air," replied Kennedy, "a very peculiar mixture - an explosive mixture."

"An explosive mixture?" echoed Orton.

"Yes, Jack, the blow-outs that you have had at the end of the tunnel were not blow-outs at all, properly speaking. They were explosions."

We sat aghast at this revelation.

"And, furthermore," added Kennedy, "I should, if I were you, call back all the men from the tunnel until the cause for the presence of this explosive mixture is discovered and remedied."

Orton reached mechanically for the telephone to give the order, but Taylor laid his hand on his arm. "One moment, Orton," he said. "Let's hear Professor Kennedy out. He may be mistaken, and there is no use frightening the men, until we are certain.

"Shelton," asked Kennedy, "what sort of flash oil is used to lubricate the machinery?"

"It is three-hundred-and-sixty-degree Fahrenheit flash test," he answered tersely.

"And are the pipes leading air down into the tunnel perfectly straight?"

"Straight?

"Yes, straight - no joints, no pockets where oil, moisture, and gases can collect."

"Straight as lines, Kennedy," he said with a sort of contemptuous defiance.

They were facing each other coldly, sizing each other up. Like a skilful lawyer, Kennedy dropped that point for a moment, to take up a new line of attack.

"Capps," he demanded, turning suddenly, "why do you always call up on the telephone and let some one know when you are going down in the tunnel and when you are coming out?"

"I don't," replied Capps, quickly recovering his composure.

"Walter," said Craig to me quietly, "go out in the outer office. Behind the telephone switchboard you will find a small box which you saw me carry in there this morning and connect with the switchboard. Detach the wires, as you saw me attach them, and bring it here."

No one moved, as I placed the box on a drafting-table before them. Craig opened it. Inside he disclosed a large disc of thin steel, like those used by some mechanical music-boxes, only without any perforations. He connected the wires from the box to a sort of megaphone. Then he started the disc revolving.

Out of the little megaphone horn, sticking up like a miniature talking-machine, came a voice: Number please. Four four three o, Yorkville. Busy, I'll call you. Try them again, Central. Hello, hello, Central - "

Kennedy stopped the machine. "It must be further along on the disc," he remarked. "This, by the way, is an instrument known as the telegraphone, invented by a Dane named Poulsen. It records conversations over a telephone on this plain metal disc by means of localised, minute electric charges."

Having adjusted the needle to another place on the disc he tried again. "We have here a record of the entire day's conversations over the telephone, preserved on this disc. I could wipe out the whole thing by pulling a magnet across it, but, needless to say, I wouldn't do that - yet. Listen."

This time it was Capps speaking. "Give me Mr. Shelton. Oh, Shelton, I'm going down in the south tube with those men Orton has sent nosing around here. I'll let you know when I start up again. Meanwhile - you know - don't let anything happen while I am there. Good-bye."

Capps sat looking defiantly at Kennedy, as he stopped the telegraphone.

"Now," continued Kennedy suavely, "what could happen? I'll answer my own question by telling what actually did happen. Oil that was smoky at a lower point than its flash was being used in the machinery - not really three-hundred-and-sixty-degree oil. The water-jacket had been tampered with, too. More than that, there is a joint in the pipe leading down into the tunnel, where explosive gases can collect. It is a well-known fact in the use of compressed air that such a condition is the best possible way to secure an explosion.

"It would all seem so natural, even if discovered," explained Kennedy rapidly. "The smoking oil - smoking just as an automobile often does - is passed into the compressed-air pipe. Condensed oil, moisture, and gases collect in the joint, and perhaps they line the whole distance of the pipe.

A spark from the low-grade oil-and they are ignited. What takes place is the same thing that occurs in the cylinder of an automobile where the air is compressed with gasoline vapour. Only here we have compressed air charged with vapour of oil. The flame proceeds down the pipe - exploding through the pipe, if it happens to be not strong enough. This pipe, however, is strong. Therefore, the flame in this case shoots out at the open end of the pipe, down near the shield, and if the air in the tunnel happens also to be surcharged with oil-vapour, an explosion takes place in the tunnel - the river bottom is blown out - then God help the sand-hogs!

"That's how your accidents took place, Orton," concluded Kennedy in triumph, "and that impure air - not impure from carbon dioxide, but from this oil-vapour mixture - increased the liability of the men for the bends. Capps knew about it. He was careful while he was there to see that the air was made as pure as possible under the circumstances. He was so careful that he wouldn't even let Mr. Jameson smoke in the tunnel. But as soon as he went to the surface, the same deadly mixture was pumped down again - I caught some of it in this flask, and - "

"My God, Paddy's down there now," cried Orton, suddenly seizing his telephone. "Operator, give me the south tube - quick - what - they don't answer?"

Out in the river above the end of the heading, where a short time before there had been only a few bubbles on the surface of the water, I could see what looked like a huge geyser of water spouting up. I pulled Craig over to me and pointed.

A blow-out," cried Kennedy, as he rushed to the door, only to be met by a group of blanched-faced workers who had come breathless to the office to deliver the news.

Craig acted quickly. "Hold these men," he ordered, pointing to Capps and Shelton, "until we come back. Orton, while we are gone, go over the entire day's record on the telegraphone. I suspect you and Miss Taylor will find something there that will interest you."

He sprang down the ladder to the tunnel air-lock, not waiting for the elevator. In front of the closed door of the lock, an excited group of men was gathered. One of them was peering through the dim, thick, glass porthole in the door.

"There he is, standin' by the door with a club, an' the men's crowdin' so fast that they're all wedged so's none can get in at all. He's beatin' 'em back with the stick. Now, he's got the door clear and has dragged one poor fellow in. It's Jimmy Rourke, him with the eight childer. Now he's dragged in a Polack. Now he's fightin' back a big Jamaica nigger who's tryin' to shove ahead of a little Italian."

"It's Paddy," cried Craig. "If he can bring them all out safely without the loss of a life he'll save the day yet for Orton. And he'll do it, too, Walter."

Instantly I reconstructed in my mind the scene in the tunnel - the explosion of the oil-vapour, the mad race up the tube, perhaps the failure of the emergency curtain to work, the frantic efforts of the men, in panic, all to crowd through the narrow little door at once; the rapidly rising water - and above all the heroic Paddy, cool to the last, standing at the door and single-handed beating the men back with a club, so that they could go through one at a time.

Only when the water had reached the level of the door of the lock, did Paddy bang it shut as he dragged the last man in. Then followed an interminable wait for the air in the lock to be exhausted. When, at last, the door at our end of the lock swung open, the men with a cheer seized Paddy and, in spite of his struggles, hoisted him on to their shoulders, and carried him off, still struggling, in triumph up the construction elevator to the open air above.

The scene in Orton's office was dramatic as the men entered with Paddy. Vivian Taylor was standing defiantly, with burning eyes, facing Capps, who stared sullenly at the floor before him. Shelton was plainly abashed.

"Kennedy," cried Orton, vainly trying to rise, "listen. Have you still that place on the telegraphone record, Vivian?"

Miss Taylor started the telegraphone, while we all crowded around leaning forward eagerly.

"Hello. Inter-River? Is this the president's office? Oh, hello. This is Capps talking. How are you? Oh, you've heard about Orton, have you? Not so bad, eh? Well, I'm arranging with my man Shelton here for the final act this afternoon. After that you can compromise with the Five-Borough on your own terms. I think I have argued Taylor and Morris into the right frame of mind for it, if we have one more big accident. What's that? How is my love affair? Well, Orton's in the way yet, but you know why I went into this deal. When you put me into his place after the compromise, I think I will pull strong with her. Saw her last night. She feels pretty bad about Orton, but she'll get over it. Besides, the pater will never let her marry a man who's down and out. By the way, you've got to do something handsome for Shelton. All right. I'll see you to-night and tell you some more. Watch the papers in the meantime for the grand finale. Good-bye."

An angry growl rose from one or two of the more quick-witted men. Kennedy reached over and pulled me with him quickly through the crowd.

"Hurry, Walter," he whispered hoarsely, "hustle Shelton and Capps out quick before the rest of the men wake up to what it's all about, or we shall have a lynching instead of an arrest."

As we shoved and pushed them out, I saw the rough and grimy sand-hogs in the rear move quickly aside, and off came their muddy, frayed hats. A dainty figure flitted among them toward Orton. It was Vivian Taylor.

"Papa," she cried, grasping Jack by both hands and turning to Taylor, who followed her closely, "Papa, I told you not to be too hasty with Jack."